Ms. Karen Bartell
745 Weatherbee Rd
Baltimore MD 21286

Plum Jam

4 lbs of stoned plums
4 lbs of sugar
½ a pint of water.

Simmer the plums
in the water until
soft. Add the sugar
and stir until
dissolved. Boil
until the jam will
set.
Put into clean warm
jars and seal well.

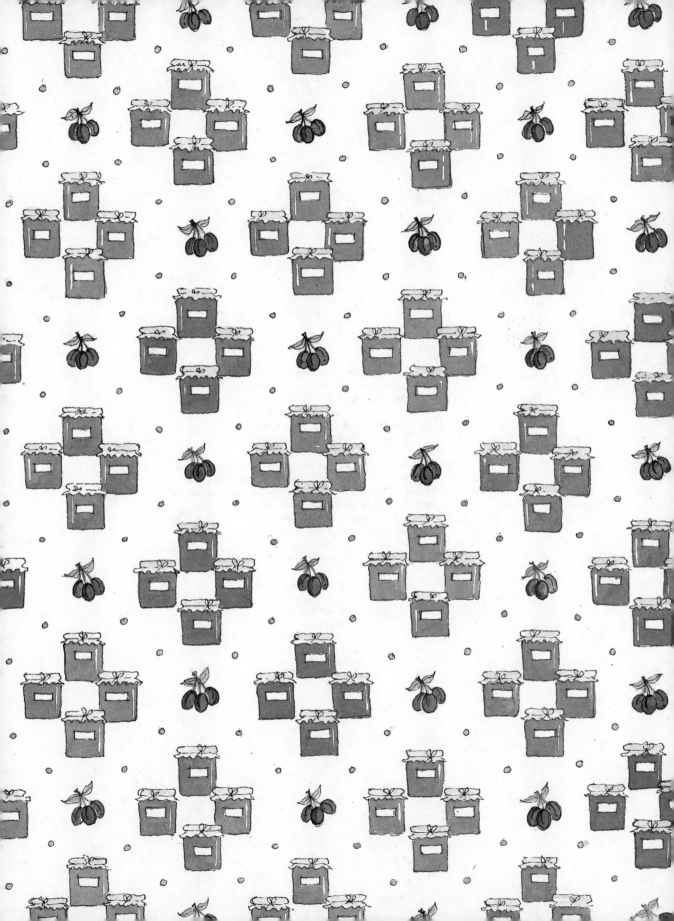

Published by The Trumpet Club
a division of Bantam Doubleday Dell Publishing Group, Inc.
666 Fifth Avenue, New York, New York 10103

Text copyright © 1985 by Margaret Mahy
Illustrations copyright © 1985 by Helen Craig

ISBN: 0-440-84231-X

This edition published by arrangement with
Little, Brown and Company Inc.
Printed in the United States of America
March 1990

10 9 8 7 6 5 4 3 2 1
UPC

JAM

A TRUE STORY

MARGARET MAHY

ILLUSTRATED BY HELEN CRAIG

A TRUMPET CLUB SPECIAL EDITION

Mr. and Mrs. Castle lived in a white house with a big, green lawn. Their three children were called Clement, Clarissa, and Carlo.

"Three little Castles," said Mr. Castle, "but very small ones—more like Cottages, really."

Mrs. Castle was studying to be an atomic scientist.

"What a clever one *she* is," said Mr. Castle. "If she decided to go to the moon I don't think she'd even need a rocket to get there."

One day Mrs. Castle announced that she had
found herself a job. Important scientists were devel-
oping an electronic medicine to cure sunspots, and
they had sent for Mrs. Castle.

"But who is going to look after us?" asked Clement.

"Isn't anyone going to be here when we come
home from school?" asked Clarissa. Carlo was too
young to say anything, but he looked worried.

"*I* shall be here, my dear little Cottages," Mr.
Castle cried. "You have no reason to be anxious."

He washed and dried
the dishes.

He swept the house from top
to bottom.

He vacuumed the carpets, put the
dough to rise in a warm place.

wiped down the counter, had
a quick cup of tea.

planted a row of cabbages,
folded the wash, baked
the bread *and* a cake...

put Carlo down for his
afternoon sleep...

had another cup of tea…

cleaned the bath…

prepared dinner…

read the paper…

kissed the children when they came home from school—and
Mrs. Castle when she came home from work—and asked them
all what sort of day they had had.

Then he gave Mrs. Castle something to drink, handed her the paper, and took the children out for a game on the big, green lawn. He was an excellent housefather.

Indeed, he was so good that one day he actually ran out of work. While he tried to think of just what to do next, there came a soft thud on the roof, and then another one.

"Sunspots!" cried Mr. Castle, and ran outside. It was not the sound of falling sunspots he had heard, but ripe plums tumbling off the old plum tree that grew behind the house.

Mr. Castle was delighted. Gathering up the fallen
plums he made three pots of plum jam.

"Jam! What a treat!" the children cried.

The next day many more plums fell from the tree
and Mr. Castle made twenty pots of plum jam.

The following day the ground under the tree was covered with big, purple plums. That day Mr. Castle had enough plums to make thirty pots of jam.

But the day after that there were even more plums. Mr. Castle had run out of jam jars.

"What a challenge!" he cried. "Not a single plum must be wasted."

He filled all the vases in the house with jam. He filled all the glasses, too. Even Carlo's rabbit mug and the teapot were filled with jam.

"The whole house is like a jam factory," said Clement.

"It's like a school for jam pots," said Clarissa.

"Your father is a born artist," said Mrs. Castle. "He is the Picasso of jam makers."

"Now all the work is done," said Mr. Castle, looking pleased. "We can look forward to eating this delicious jam all year long."

They began with jam sandwiches. Mrs. Castle,
Clement, and Clarissa had jam sandwiches in the
lunches Mr. Castle prepared for them every morning. Carlo, who was cutting new teeth, had jam on
his crusts.

"Hooray!" called Mr. Castle. "We've emptied the teapot already. We'll be able to have tea with our cakes, cookies, and tarts."

That winter the roof leaked a little. Mr. Castle's jam proved very useful, for as well as being delicious, it stopped leaks. When the tiles came off the bathroom floor, Mr. Castle stuck them down again with jam. After weeks of devoted jam eating they could put flowers in the vases again, and drink from glasses instead of from eggcups.

"I wouldn't really care if I never saw another pot of jam in my life," Clarissa whispered to Clement. "But don't tell Daddy I said so."

In the meantime they had jam with everything, and on everything, and under everything. Their dreams became haunted with jam. Clement dreamed that the sky opened and jam rained down on him. Clarissa dreamed of fat, shadowy jam pots marching through the night, crying out a terrible war cry of "Jam! Jam! Jam!"

Mrs. Castle dreamed that it was proved that sun-spots were caused by too much jam, and Carlo dreamed great jammy dreams as well. Their days were full of jam eating, and their nights of dreams all dripping with jam.

Finally, one morning Mr. Castle went to the cupboard to get down the next pot of jam only to find it was empty. There was not a single potful left.

"Let's have egg sandwiches for lunch," said Mrs. Castle.

"Let's have fish and chips," suggested Clement.

"Spaghetti and salad," cried Clarissa.

!

"But first let's have a game on the lawn," said Mr. Castle. "We've eaten so much jam that we look like jam pots ourselves. We shall have to get back in shape."

While they were playing on the lawn, Mr. Castle heard a soft thud on the roof.

The plums were ripe again.

Plum Jam

4 lbs of stoned plums
4 lbs of sugar
½ a pint of water.

Simmer the plums
in the water until
soft. Add the sugar
and stir until
dissolved. Boil
until the jam will
set.
Put into clean warm
jars and seal well.